# Becoming Brave
# How Little Buffalo Finds Courage

Cows run away from the storm while the buffalo
charges toward it – and gets through it quicker.

Whenever I'm confronted with a tough challenge,
I do not prolong the torment, I become the buffalo.
~ Wilma Mankiller

# Becoming Brave
# How Little Buffalo Finds Courage

## Jed Jurchenko

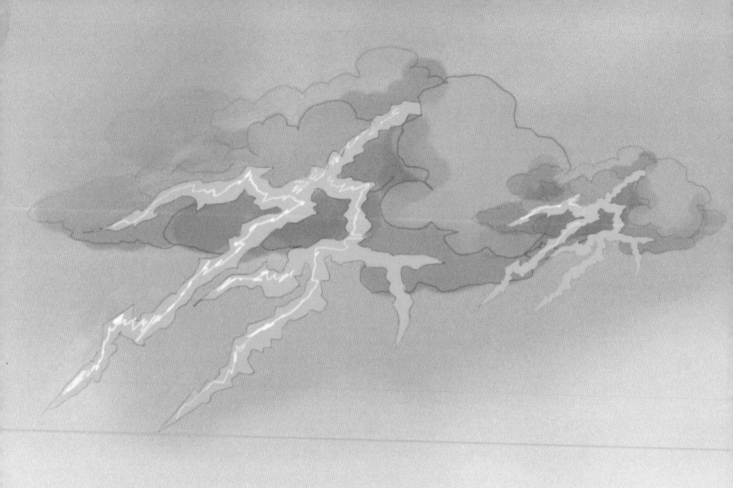

Dark clouds loomed on the horizon, and thunder echoed across the grassy plain.

Suddenly, a burst of lightning flashed across the sky, causing Little Buffalo to shudder.

A mighty storm was on its way. The tiny buffalo was afraid, and his heart beat rapidly.
He did not feel prepared for the challenges ahead.

As the young buffalo nuzzled nervously
against his mother's side,
his thoughts wandered
back to when life was peaceful.

Only yesterday, the sun was bright. Birds chirped. Rabbits and deer scampered about a nearby forest. Little Buffalo grazed lazily, without a care in the world.

After pulling up a mouthful of grass,
Little Buffalo noticed his father sniff the air.
Following Dad's lead, Little Buffalo sniffed too.
"Son," his father asked in his burly voice,
"Can you feel the moisture in the air?
Do you see the heavy clouds
forming on the horizon?
These are signs that a storm is on the way."

The young buffalo had never seen a storm and asked, "Father, what is that?"
"Storms bring hardship and danger," his father replied.
"There are strong winds, icy rains, and lightning that is powerful enough to knock a
buffalo off of his feet." Little Buffalo gasped. "Then we should hide?" he asked.
"No," Dad replied. "We are mighty Buffalo. Unlike other animals, we run into the storm.
Tomorrow, we will charge toward the wind and rain.
We will keep running until we reach the other side!"

"But Dad, that storm looks dangerous.
Why do we have to run into it?"
Little Buffalo asked nervously.
"Ah yes... I wondered the same thing when
I was your age," Dad replied.

"Buffalo run into the storm because
it is the fastest way to reach the beauty on the other side.
Once you have run through this storm, you will understand."

Boom!
The thunder grew louder and shook the ground.

"Dad?" little buffalo asked nervously, "What if I am not strong enough to reach the other side?"

"Some storms are too strong for a buffalo to face alone.
This is why we always run together. But now, you must
stop asking questions and prepare for the run.
Start by taking three deep breaths.
Quiet your body, and hold your head high.
Soon, we will face this storm together."

The tiny buffalo followed his father's instructions.
After taking three big breaths, he turned toward the storm.
An icy wind blasted into his face.
Although his body trembled, Little Buffalo continued to
breathe deeply and tried his best to remain calm.

A single droplet of water splashed onto Little Buffalo's nose.
"It is time to run!" Dad proclaimed.
"Little Buffalo, you are courageous and strong.
Let's run through this storm together."

As Little Buffalo charged into the wind and rain,
the sky grew darker.
The thunder boomed louder,
and the tiny buffalo's heart grew heavy.
With no end in sight, Little Buffalo felt like giving up.
This storm is too big. I will never make it.
Little Buffalo thought to himself.

That was when his father's words came to mind.
As Little Buffalo focused on these new thoughts,
he felt stronger. He placed one hoof in front of the other
and pressed forward.

After what felt like an eternity, the downpour softened.
A golden beam of sunlight broke through the clouds,
guiding the way better than any lighthouse.

When the rain stopped, so did the buffalo herd.
Little Buffalo and his family had reached the other side.
A green pasture glistened in the glorious sunlight.
A beautiful rainbow stretched across the sky.
"Son," dad said proudly, "Breath in the fresh air,
and always remember this moment.
Incredible beauty is on the other side of the storm."

Little buffalo soaked in the
brilliant sights, sounds, and smells.
He finally understood why
buffalo run into the storm.

How To Be Brave
and
Run Through Your Storm!

Identify Your Storm

Kids face different kinds of storms than buffalos.
What storm do you need to run through?


Learning a difficult sport or skill.
Moving to a new house or school.
Making new friends.
Learning not to be afraid of the dark.
Feeling sick, getting hurt, or having surgery.
Being bullied by other children.
Having a parent leave on deployment, separate, or divorce.
Living with grandparents or in a foster home.

# Take Big, Deep, Buffalo Breaths

Buffalo breaths help kids to calm their body and mind.

1. Sit up straight, with your feet on the floor, and one hand on your belly.

2. Breathe in through your nose. Fill your tummy with air, like a beach ball.

3. Exhale slowly, through your mouth. Push all of the air out of your belly.

4. Repeat this at least three times. If you feel your body relaxing, then you are doing it right.

# Think Like a Buffalo

Repeat these buffalo-thoughts as you move forward.

1. I am brave, and I am strong.
2. I have done hard things before, and I can do hard things again.
3. Running through the storm is the fastest way to the other side.
4. My friends and family will help me.
5. I can make good choices. I am in charge of me.

These thoughts are helpful because they are true! Which thoughts will encourage you the most as you run through your storm?

# Stick With Your Herd

Identify your buffalo herd and stick with them!

1. A family member who believes in me is_____.
2. My best friend is_____.
3. An adult who can help me at school is_____.
4. A friend who makes me smile is_____.
5. An adult who will give me good advice is_____.

Remember, buffalo always run together!

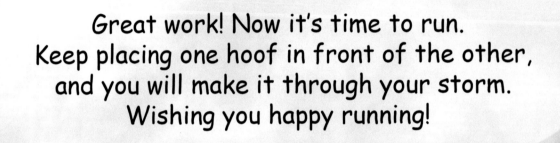